For James and his animals ✦ **B.S.**

For my parents
And with thanks to Chris Lewin and the Hurlburt family ✦ **W.M.**

First published 1995 by Walker Books Ltd
87 Vauxhall Walk, London SE11 5HJ

This edition published 1996

2 4 6 8 10 9 7 5 3 1

Text © 1995 Brenda Seabrooke
Illustrations © 1995 Wenhai Ma

This book has been typeset in Centaur.

Printed in Hong Kong

British Library Cataloguing in Publication Data
A catalogue record for this book is available
from the British Library.

ISBN 0-7445-4070-4

THE Swan's Gift

Written by

BRENDA SEABROOKE

Illustrated by

WENHAI MA

WALKER BOOKS
AND SUBSIDIARIES
LONDON • BOSTON • SYDNEY

Anton was a farmer who lived with his wife Rubina and their seven children at the edge of a forest. He worked hard and they were happy for many years. Then one spring the rains didn't fall and Anton's wheat died in the fields.

✦ As winter came on, their food supply grew smaller and smaller.

Soon Anton's shoulders were stooped with worry. Rubina's plump apple cheeks withered. The children no longer sang or laughed or danced, for they were all too hungry.

➤ Every day Anton went out
to look for game but returned
without firing a shot. And every
day Rubina added water to the
onion soup until there was
nothing in the pot but water.
When Anton saw his family
crying with hunger he wanted
to cry too. But instead he took
his gun and went out again into
the cold cold night.

➤ He had to find something for them to eat: a bird or a rabbit. But the black branches were empty of birds and no rabbits crouched in the frozen scrub. The only tracks Anton saw were his own.

He came to a small hill and knew it was the last one he would be able to climb before his strength was gone. His feet were numb and his breath rasped in the freezing air. At the top of the rise he stopped to rest, scanning the snow for animal tracks.

➤ In despair Anton turned to go. Just then he saw below him a lake that had not yet frozen over. Its edge was lacy with ice and at its centre floated a swan of such dazzling beauty that Anton could not look away. Its stark white feathers gleamed against the dark water and as Anton watched, the swan seemed to grow larger until its image filled his eyes.

→ Suddenly juices flowed into Anton's mouth. He could taste succulent roast swan and see his children's faces glowing as his family sat at the table eating again. He raised his gun and sighted down the long barrel.

Anton put his finger on the trigger. The swan seemed to be looking at him, listening for the shot that would kill it.

❧ He lowered the gun. The swan was the most beautiful
creature Anton had ever seen. As he watched, the swan
fanned its magnificent wings in a way that seemed to
embrace the night. Anton closed his eyes and thought of
his family. Again he raised the gun.

➤ Hours seemed to pass. The feathers on the swan's breast moved gently with each beat of its heart, and Anton could feel his own heart beating. He lifted his heavy wet feet, walked a few steps, and then dropped to his knees.

"I can't do it," he said.

"Why not?" asked a voice as soft as snow or feathers ruffling in a gentle wind.

"I cannot kill beauty. If I kill this swan my family will have food for one or two meals. And then what? We will be hungry again and it will have been for nothing."

Anton was too tired to be surprised that he was speaking to the swan or the wind or the night. He was too tired to walk back home. He bowed his head with sadness for his family.

➤ With a cry the swan lifted its wings, rose from the lake, and circled over Anton, water dropping from its wing feathers. As the water hit the snow it froze into crystals that sparkled in the moonlight. Anton reached out and touched one. It was hard, harder than ice, and did not melt in the warmth of his hand.

"A diamond!" Anton said.

Quickly he scooped up the diamonds that lay in a glittering circle around him. He filled his pockets with them and set off through the snow to a nearby village.

✤ Anton was no longer tired. He no longer felt the cold. He woke up the innkeeper, calling, "I need food."

"Your crops failed," said the innkeeper. "Everyone knows you have no money."

"I have a diamond," said Anton.

"Where would the likes of you get a diamond?" the man scoffed.

"Let me in and I will explain."

The innkeeper fed Anton cold venison and sweet dumplings while Anton told his story, and the innkeeper's wife packed a sledge for him with roast chickens and cheeses and onions and turnips. Then they sent Anton on his way so that they could begin looking for the magic swan themselves.

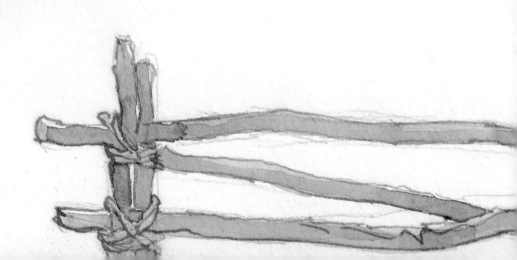

➤ Rubina met him at the door. "Did you find any game? Mischa has fainted."

"No. But look what I have brought." Anton showed her the sledge.

"But how did you get it?" she asked.

For answer, he spilled the diamonds onto the table.

"Oh," cried Rubina, "you have turned to robbery!"

"No," said Anton. And he told her all about the swan, and how it had circled him with diamonds falling from its wings.

✢ Anton and Rubina woke the children even though it was the middle of the night, and they all sat at the table eating slowly, enjoying the flavour of the food and the wonderful feeling in their stomachs. Rubina's black eyes sparkled as she filled her children's bowls. Anton felt his strength returning. Several of the children hummed as they were put to bed.

➤ Anton and Rubina and their children prospered, for they used their diamonds wisely and well. News of the magic swan spread throughout the land and many people searched for it. But the swan was never found.

Sometimes when Anton was alone in the forest the image of the swan rose before him. He saw again the gleam of its feathers, the coral glow of its beak, and the magnificent reach of its wings as it glided silently across the sky.

MORE WALKER PAPERBACKS
For You to Enjoy

THE MOUSEHOLE CAT
by Antonia Barber/Nicola Bayley

This dramatic and moving Cornish tale of Mowzer, the cat, and Tom, the old fisherman,
who brave the fury of the Great Storm Cat, was the children's choice for the
Smarties Book Prize and winner of the British Book Award (Illustrated Children's Book of the Year).
Shown several times on television, it's now available on video, too.

"A glorious tale... A book to wallow in, read and re-read,
for any age from five or so to very grown-up." *The Sunday Times*

0-7445-2353-2   £4.99

THE SELFISH GIANT
by Oscar Wilde/Dom Mansell

"A classic and poignant tale... Dom Mansell's delightful illustrations
are both colourful and full of amusing detail." *BBC Radio*

0-7445-1412-6   £3.99

THE SNOW QUEEN
by Hans Christian Andersen/Angela Barrett

"Elegantly retold ... with illustrations of classic beauty." *The Observer*

0-7445-2038-X   £4.99

THE MAN WHO WANTED TO LIVE FOR EVER
retold by Selina Hastings, illustrated by Reg Cartwright

This colourful rendering of a classic European folk tale about a man's search
for the secret of eternal life is on the recommended reading list
of the National Curriculum Standard Assessment Tasks (SATs) Level 4.

"A good treatment of a good story." *The Daily Telegraph*

0-7445-2077-0   £4.99